"Go away!" I yelled. "Leave me alone!"

"But, I thought I was your favourite," it said. "You've always said so."

It was true, custard creams were my favourite biscuit, but that didn't mean I wanted to go out with a giant one, which had arms, legs and a face. Although, it *was* surprisingly handsome – for a biscuit.

"My name is Ralph." The biscuit offered its hand.

"I don't care what your name is. I'm not going out with you. Get away! Get away!"

"Jill! Jill! Wake up! Jill!"

Kathy looked concerned. "I only nipped out to the shops to get your stupid biscuits. How did you manage to fall asleep in the meantime?"

I was still trying to get my bearings. I'd called in at Kathy's for a cup of tea, and thrown a mini strop because she'd run out of custard creams. To shut me up, she'd popped out to the local store to buy some, and I must have fallen asleep.

"It sounded like you were having a nightmare," she said, switching on the kettle.

"I was. It was horrible."

"What was it about?"

"There was this – err – giant – err – I can't remember."

Kathy was already convinced I had some kind of unnatural custard cream fetish – no point in giving her more ammunition.

"There you go." She passed me the cup of tea. "And, here's your precious biscuits." Kathy offered me the packet of custard creams.

"Err — no thanks. I think I'll have a chocolate digestive instead."

My name is Jill Gooder, and I'm a P.I. My life had become much more complicated when I'd discovered that I was a witch. I wasn't allowed to tell any human about the whole *witch* thing, and that included my adoptive sister, Kathy.

I'd decided to treat myself to a few days' holiday leading up to Christmas. At least, that was my story. It might also have had something to do with the fact that I had no cases to work on. I'd told Mrs V, my PA/receptionist and knitter extraordinaire, that she should take some time off, but she wouldn't hear of it. Instead, she was manning the office just in case Santa turned up and wanted me to find his missing reindeer.

"Are you absolutely sure?" Kathy was giving me earache about something else. Nagging me seemed to be her favourite pastime.

"Positive." I reassured her.

"What are you positive about?"

"About the thing you were nagging — err — asking me about."

"And that *thing* was?"

"You know. The thing."

"You haven't been listening to a word I've said, have you?"

"I'm still in shock from the nightmare."

"Listen up. This is important. Did you buy the Total Dream Office for Lizzie for Christmas like you promised you would?"

Lizzie was my niece. Kathy had two kids: Lizzie and Mikey. I had a vague memory of Kathy saying something about which presents I should buy for them. It hadn't really been top of my list of priorities at the time. I was a busy woman: Places to go, people to meet. Anyway, why all the fuss about a silly present? I'd get around to it eventually.

"It's all in hand," I lied. "All bought and paid for."

"It had better be. Those things are like gold dust."

Yeah. Yeah. "Stop worrying. Your favourite sister has it in hand."

"Okay, but I'm trusting you. Don't let me down." Kathy took a bite of one of *my* custard creams. "Are we agreed on what we're doing over Christmas?" she said, through a mouthful of biscuit.

"Yep. All agreed. I have to come to you on Christmas Eve because you don't want to see your only sister on Christmas Day."

"That's not how it is."

It was way too easy to wind Kathy up.

"I've already explained." She sighed. "We've promised to go to Pete's mother's on Christmas Day. She said you can come too."

I'd rather chew glass with a topping of mustard.

"It's okay." I pouted. "I wouldn't want to spoil your Christmas dinner. Anyway, I hear the soup is really good at the homeless shelter."

She gave me a look.

"I'm only kidding. I'll be fine. Anyway, when does Peter break up for the holiday?"

"Don't ask. He's going away on a three-day course on tree maintenance."

"I didn't realise you had to maintain trees." I grinned. "You mean oil them and stuff?"

Kathy rolled her eyes at my stupid remark. "The course finishes on Christmas Eve, so muggins here has got to see to all the preparations by herself. Pete makes out he doesn't want to go, but I reckon he's looking forward to a few days away from me and the kids. Just him and the mini-bar."

"I could help you with the Christmas preparations."

She laughed. "Good joke."

"What's funny? I'm sure I could do something."

"No offence, Jill, but I've seen your idea of helping before. I'll be okay. Just get yourself around here on Christmas Eve evening. Pete should be back by then."

"Oh well. Don't say I didn't offer. Are the kids getting excited?"

I could still remember how I'd been as a kid on the run up to Christmas. Every day had seemed to last an eternity.

"Yeah. They're really excited about the presents, but—" She hesitated.

"What?"

"It's nothing."

"Come on. Something's up. I can tell."

"It's just Mikey. One of the kids in his class told him that Santa isn't real. I tried to convince him otherwise, but he's having none of it. I'd kind of hoped he might believe in Santa for a few more years. I guess I'm just being daft."

"What about Lizzie?"

"She still believes in him. I just hope Mikey doesn't say anything to upset her."

***

After I left Kathy's, I called in at the office. It just didn't feel right for Mrs V to be working when I was on holiday. Of course, when I say working—Mrs V actually spent most of her day knitting.

"Morning, Mrs V. Any messages?"

"Morning, Jill. Nothing at all. No visitors. No phone calls."

I was destined to always be broke.

"Oh wait. I tell a lie," she said. "There was *one* visitor."

"Really?" Hope sprang eternal.

"The landlord popped in to tell you the rent will be going up from March next year."

"Great."

"He did wish us a Merry Christmas though."

"I don't know why you don't get off home, Mrs V. It's not like anything is likely to happen here."

"I'd rather stay here, dear. Saves me using my heating. And besides, I've got a project on."

"What kind of project?"

"I've had a request to knit one hundred socks for the local children's home."

"You mean one hundred pairs?"

"No. Just one hundred individual socks. They're for the kids to hang up on Christmas Eve."

"How are you ever going to make that many?"

Mrs V was the queen of knitting, but I doubted that even she could manage to make so many in the time remaining.

"It's all in hand. I've called in a few favours from my yarnies."

Yarnies was a kind of 'street' term for Mrs V's knitting

colleagues.

"Okay. Well good luck with it." I glanced at my office. "Have you had any trouble from you-know-who?" I gestured towards the door.

"No more than usual. If I'm even five minutes late with his food, he meows the place down. You should give him to someone as a Christmas present."

I was pretty certain that no one would thank me for giving them Winky, my one-eyed, psycho cat. I'd adopted him from the cat home. At least, that was my version of events. According to him, he'd chosen me—something for which I should be eternally grateful. Either way, we were stuck with one another. Ever since I'd inherited my 'witch' powers, he'd been able to talk to me. I guess everything has its downside.

"Morning, Winky," I said, expecting the usual mixture of complaints and abuse.

He didn't even look up. He was sitting on the sofa with a pile of envelopes on either side of him. Bless—he was writing his Christmas cards.

How come my cat—who never set foot outside my office—had such a huge Christmas card list? I'd only bought a pack of ten cards, and I'd still ended up with three spare. I could only assume the cards were for the cats he'd 'met' on the social network site: FelineSocial.com. Ever since Winky's would-be girlfriend, Bella, the feline supermodel, had sent him a smartphone, he was always online.

I had no cases to work on, so there wasn't much point in my hanging around the office. The cat was busy writing his cards and my receptionist had more than enough knitting to keep her occupied. A quick visit to Candlefield was called for.

Since discovering I was a witch, I'd divided my time between Washbridge in the human world, and Candlefield, which was home to all manner of supernatural beings (*sups* for short).

***

Snow! I hadn't expected that when I magicked myself there. It came halfway up my calves. I was hardly dressed for it, in heels, a skirt and a blouse.

"Aren't you cold?" Grandma said. The woman had an annoying habit of turning up at just the wrong moment.

"I wasn't expecting snow."

"Clearly." She cackled. "You're going to get frost bite."

"Can you help me?"

"I could."

"Will you?"

"What's in it for me?"

"What about the spirit of Christmas?"

"You mean Whisky? Yes, I suppose I might be bribed—"

"No, I meant *spirit* as in being nice."

"Nah, I'd prefer Whisky."

I began to shiver uncontrollably.

"I tell you what," she said. "I'll get you out of there, and kit you out in winter gear if you agree to do me one favour in return."

"What?"

"I don't know yet. I'll let you know when I decide."

That sounded like a recipe for disaster. There had to be

another way for me to get out. I didn't need Grandma. I could use magic to levitate out of the snow. I'd show her.

I closed my eyes and focussed on the spell. Nothing! I tried again. Still nothing.

Grandma had an evil look on her face—she was doing something to block my magic.

"What are you doing?" I yelled at her. "Why won't my spells work?"

"Me? I'm just standing here, minding my own business."

I tried again. It was hopeless. I had no other option but to accept her offer of help.

"Okay, okay. I agree. I'll owe you *one* favour. Now will you help me, please?"

"With a snap of her fingers, I was free, and dressed in clothing suitable for a Polar expedition. Every part of me was snuggly warm. But at what price I wondered? Grandma gave an extra evil cackle as she disappeared.

"Jill, you look like an Eskimo." Amber was behind the counter in Cuppy C.

"Help me out of this will you?" I said. "I'm cooking inside here."

"I like your boots. Where did you get them?"

"Grandma gave me all this gear."

"Grandma?" Amber couldn't have looked any more surprised if I'd told her that it had fallen out of the sky.

"Well not *gave* exactly. I had to promise to do her a favour in return."

"You didn't agree, did you? Please tell me you didn't."

"What choice did I have? It was that or get frost bite."

"Frost bite would have been better. Trust me."

What had I done?

Chapter 2

Cuppy C was almost deserted.

"It's been like this ever since it started to snow," Amber said, as she joined me at a window table.

"Where's Pearl?"

Amber and Pearl were my twin cousins. The two of them ran Cuppy C, a cake shop and tea room. The only time they weren't squabbling was when they were asleep.

"She's Christmas shopping."

"In this weather?"

"Nothing gets between Pearl and a shopping expedition." Amber took a sip of coffee. "Same for me, I guess. We agreed to have one day off each. It's my turn tomorrow. I hope the weather has improved by then."

"It looks unlikely. Do you still have much to get?"

"Not really. Just a few last minute presents. I did my main Christmas shop last week. I've got a fantastic present for Mum. She'll love it."

"I had planned to go and see Aunt Lucy later, but I'm not sure I'll bother in this."

Outside, the snow had begun to fall again.

"Probably just as well. She's stressed to the max."

"Why?"

"About Christmas dinner. It's all Grandma's fault."

"I might have guessed. Has she been criticising your mum's cooking again?" That was one of grandma's favourite pastimes.

"Not exactly, but she says Mum should use magic to make the Christmas dinner, and Mum insists she wants to do it the traditional way."

Although I wouldn't admit it, I was with Grandma on

this one. Why spend all that time and energy on making dinner when you could simply cast a spell? Seemed like a no-brainer to me.

"So is Aunt Lucy sticking to her guns?"

"So far, but Grandma is like a dog with a bone."

"What was that?" I almost jumped out of my skin when something thudded against the window.

"It's Miles!" Amber snarled. "I'm going to kill him."

Miles Best had been at school with the twins. Back then, they'd both had a crush on him, but the years had not been kind to him. He and his girlfriend, Mindy, had opened up a competing cake shop, Best Cakes, directly across the road from Cuppy C.

"What's he playing at?" I said, as another snowball hit the window.

"I don't know." Amber's face was red with rage. "But, I'm going to teach him a lesson."

"Wait! Do you think that's a good idea?"

It was too late. She'd already grabbed her coat and boots, and was headed for the door. If I'm honest, I would rather have remained a spectator, but when I saw Mindy join Miles, I knew I had to help Amber.

"This is silly," I shouted. "Can't we all just be adults? Ouch!" The snowball caught me on my shoulder. Miles was grinning all over his face. Right, this was war.

I probably shouldn't have used the 'power' spell for something so puerile, but hey, all's fair in love and snowball fights. I caught Miles in the midriff with a *power* snowball. Amber took one on the arm.

The snowballs were flying back and forth across the deserted street, and there was no sign of either side backing down.

Just then, Grandma poked her head out of Cuppy C. "Is there any danger of getting served in here?"

A snowball caught her square on the nose.

It was as if time stood still. All four of us stared at Grandma—the throbbing wart on her nose was mesmerising. The only sound to be heard was me trying desperately to suppress a laugh.

If there's one thing I admire about Grandma, it's her magic skillz. She makes it all look so effortless. If I hadn't known she was responsible, I would have thought that the avalanche which engulfed Best Cakes had been an act of nature.

Miles and Mindy were buried up to their waists in snow. Amber broke the silence.

"Need a hand, Miles?"

"Yes. Get me out!"

"Sorry, too busy."

Amber and I couldn't stop laughing as we returned to our coffee and cup-cakes. We spent the next hour watching Miles and his girlfriend digging themselves and their shop out.

"We shouldn't laugh." I laughed.

"That must be hard work." Amber giggled.

Just then, the door flew open.

"Give me a hand, you two!" Pearl shouted. She was weighed down with bags.

We took some of them from her as she shook the snow from her hair.

"What happened across the road?" Pearl made herself a coffee, and joined us at the window table.

"Grandma happened." Amber grinned.

"Miles must have done something really bad to make her so mad."

Amber looked around to make sure it was safe to talk. "It was so funny," she said. "He hit her right on the end of her nose with a snowball."

Amber's laugh was cut short when a huge lump of snow appeared from nowhere, and dropped onto her head.

Pearl and I screamed with laughter.

While Amber was drying her hair, Pearl whispered, "I've got the best ever present for Mum."

"What is it?"

"I can't tell you. I want it to be a surprise."

"I won't tell her."

"Sorry, it's top secret."

"Where's Barry," I shouted downstairs. Barry was my adorable, if a bit dim, labradoodle. He normally came running to greet me whenever I went up to my room above Cuppy C.

"He's under your bed," Pearl shouted from the bottom of the stairs. "He's scared of the snow."

"I thought dogs were meant to love snow?"

"Not this one. We've tried to take him a walk a couple of times, but he wouldn't set foot on it. We had to clear a small area around the back so he could go out and do his business."

I got down on all fours, and looked under the bed.

"Barry? What are you doing there?"

"Don't like the white."

"It's only snow."

"Don't like it."

"It's just rain, but colder."

"It's white."

"It can't hurt you."

"Don't like it."

"We could go to the park."

Barry loved the park more than anything except dog biscuits, and even then it was a close call.

"Is it white there?"

"There's snow everywhere."

"Don't like it."

I could see I was fighting a losing battle.

"Any luck?" Amber asked when I went back down to the shop.

"He won't budge. How can a dog be scared of snow?"

"Barry's scared of his own shadow. He's a big wuss."

Maybe, but he was *my* big wuss, and I didn't like to see him so upset. I'd have to figure out a way of helping him to overcome his 'white' phobia.

"You're coming over for Christmas dinner aren't you, Jill?" Pearl was cashing up for the day. They had given up hope of seeing any more customers.

"Try stopping me. I wouldn't miss Aunt Lucy's Christmas dinner for anything."

"What about your sister? Doesn't she want you to go to her place?"

"I'm going to Kathy's on Christmas Eve. They're going to Peter's mother's on Christmas Day."

"I love Christmas at Mum's," Pearl said. "Except for one thing." She glanced all around her.

We knew what she was thinking, but after what had just happened to Amber, none of us were going to say the word aloud. I had no doubt Grandma would be there on Christmas Day, and would do her best to put a damper on celebrations, but I was determined I wouldn't let her spoil it for me.

"Are you going to bring Drake?" Amber said.

"I doubt it. He probably has his own family stuff to do."

"But you two are okay, aren't you?"

"Yeah. We're just friends, I guess."

"Is that all?"

"Looks that way."

I didn't really know where I stood with Drake. He was a wizard who I'd met while walking Barry. We'd hit it off straight away, and we'd been out a couple of times—not exactly dates, but close.

***

That evening, I was back in Washbridge, and a little overdressed. I was still sporting the outfit which Grandma had magicked up for me. Problem was, there was zero snow. In fact, it was quite mild for the time of year. As I made my way back home, I drew a few strange looks from people wondering why an Eskimo was on the streets of Washbridge.

As I walked past the shop which was close to my block of flats, I noticed they had mistletoe for sale, and I had a brilliant idea.

Luther Stone's flat was on the floor above mine. He was my accountant—I know what you're thinking, but you're wrong. He wasn't your run of the mill accountant—Luther was scorching hot. So, I got to thinking: what if *someone* was to hang mistletoe outside the door to my flat. And, what if I happened to step out of my door just as Luther was walking by? What do you mean it smacked of desperation? It *was* tradition, and I'm nothing if not a traditionalist.

I grabbed a stool from the kitchen, and quickly checked the corridor to make sure the coast was clear.

After hanging the mistletoe, I went back into my flat and waited. Luther had a habit of singing to himself, and wouldn't you know it, that man could carry a tune. Just then, I heard him coming—this was my big chance. Nonchalant was the name of the game. I'd open the door, see Luther, and then look surprised at the mistletoe above our heads. What could possibly go wrong?

Betty?

Betty Longbottom, another one of my neighbours, was standing directly in front of me; she was staring at Luther who had just noticed the mistletoe.

No! That was *my* mistletoe!

"Hello, Betty." Luther smouldered. "Looks like you've caught me under the mistletoe."

Betty glanced up, and had the audacity to pretend she hadn't realised.

What an actress! She knew exactly what she was doing. Stealing *my* mistletoe kiss—that's what she was doing. The harlot! The hussy!

Luther planted a kiss on Betty's lips. Her cheeks lit up and I thought she was going to faint.

"Hi, Jill," Luther said, as he went on his way.

Hi? Is that all I get? What about *my* kiss under *my* mistletoe?

Betty seemed to recover, and for the first time noticed I was standing there.

"Oh, hello, Jill."

I didn't speak. Instead, I went back into my flat, and slammed the door closed. Not that I was bitter or anything.

Chapter 3

I'd never understood why people bought Christmas presents so early in the year. Kathy usually started sometime in August. Me? I didn't give it a thought until well into December, but I always got the job done. It was all about planning and organisation.

The shop assistant laughed in my face. How unprofessional.

"Total Dream Office?" She managed through fits of laughter.

I had no idea why she should find that so funny. "Yes. Could you gift wrap it for me, please?"

"Gift wrap it?" She dissolved into laughter again.

I wasn't the vindictive sort, but I was seriously considering reporting her to the store manager. This simply wasn't acceptable.

"I'm sorry." She wiped tears from her eyes. She didn't look very sorry.

"I *am* in rather a hurry," I said.

"We haven't had a Total Dream Office for over a week."

"When will you be getting more in?"

"Your guess is as good as mine, but not this side of Christmas."

How annoying. I'd chosen this shop because it was en-route to the office. I'd planned to call in on Mrs V to make sure she was okay.

"Where's the nearest shop I can buy one?"

"You won't find one. It's one of this year's bestsellers. I bought one for my niece a few weeks ago. No one has any stock left."

Oh no. Oh no, no, no. I'd told Kathy I'd already bought one.

"What about online?"

"Same." She shrugged.

"What about the auction web sites? Someone must be selling them on."

"Possibly. Last I heard, they were asking ten times the list price, and I believe some of them are counterfeit."

"Ten times the list price?" The stupid thing was already a ludicrous price. "Do you have anything which is like it?"

"Not really. It's kind of a one-off."

I was dead. Kathy would tear open my chest and rip out my heart. Literally.

Breathe, Jill—I mustn't panic. There was still time, and while there was time, there was hope.

I hoped.

As I climbed the stairs, I could hear numerous voices. The outer office was full of women—plus a solitary man; they were all knitting. I managed to weave my way through to Mrs V.

"Morning, Jill. You don't mind if I knit while we talk do you? We're up against a deadline here."

"Sure. Carry on. I was just surprised to find so many people in the office."

"I told you I was going to get my yarnies to help with the children's home project."

"You did. I just hadn't realised that they were all going to come into the office."

"I figured it would be better this way. We can encourage one another." She looked up from the knitting. "Ladies, this is Jill Gooder, my boss."

Someone coughed.

"Sorry Cecil. I forgot you'd joined us today. I should have said, Ladies and *Gentleman*. This is Jill."

I managed a smile.

"Jill has kindly allowed us to use the office for our project."

"Well, it is for a good cause." I felt obliged to say something. "I wish you all well with your knitting."

Just then, Kathy appeared in the doorway. She saw all the yarnies, and gave me a puzzled look. Rather than try to explain, I beckoned her to follow me through to my office.

"What's going on out there?" She said, once I'd closed the door.

"Never mind about all that!" Winky said, as he jumped onto my desk. "I haven't been fed yet."

Fortunately, all Kathy could hear was a series of meows.

"I'll have to feed him or we'll never get any peace."

"I don't understand why you keep that stupid cat. He can't be good for business."

"Who does she think she is?" Winky said while gobbling his food. "I've a good mind to sharpen my claws on her fat legs."

"Don't you dare!"

"Dare what?" Kathy looked at me as though I'd lost my mind—again.

"Err—nothing—it was the cat—I thought he was going to—err—never mind."

I glanced down at her legs—maybe she had put on a little weight?

"Why are you staring at my legs?"

"I wasn't."

"Do you think they're getting fat?"

"Fat? No, of course not."

"They're like tree trunks!" Winky shouted, as he started on his full-cream milk.

"So what's going on out there?" Kathy said. "Is business so bad that you've started hiring out the room?"

"No." Although that might not be such a bad idea. "They're just Mrs V's yarnies."

"Yarnies?"

"Come on, Kathy. You've got to get down with the street talk. They're her friends from the knitting club. Mrs V has promised to knit a hundred socks for the children's home for Christmas."

"A hundred pairs?"

"No. A hundred single socks apparently. They're for the kids to hang up on Christmas Eve."

"It's a good cause, I guess, but isn't it interfering with your business? What do your clients make of it?"

What clients?

"It's okay. I've decided to take a few days off. I just popped in to check on Mrs V, and to feed the cat. What brings you here, anyway?"

"Your grandmother asked me to come over to tell you and Mrs V about the Christmas party at Ever. You're both invited."

'Ever' was short for Ever A Wool Moment which was Grandma's wool emporium.

"When is it?"

"The day before Christmas Eve. Lunch time onwards."

"I guess I'll be there then. It's not like I have a choice." I sighed. "Are the kids getting excited about the big day?"

"Lizzie is beside herself. She keeps asking how many

minutes there are left."

"I imagine she'll be getting tons of presents."

"Probably, but there's only one she's really bothered about."

Oh no!

"She never stops talking about it."

Oh no!

"I don't see what all the fuss is about, but all the other girls in her class are getting one too."

Oh no!

"It's a good job you bought it when you did because you can't get Total Dream Office now for love nor money."

"Yeah — good job I did."

I should have owned up right there and then, but I was too much of a coward.

"I can't wait to see her face when she opens it." Kathy smiled.

I was so dead.

"I'm a bit upset with Mikey though." Her smile faded.

"What's he done?"

"He told Lizzie that Santa wasn't real."

"Did she get upset?"

"No. Lizzie told him he didn't know what he was talking about, and that he wouldn't be getting any toys for being naughty."

"Good for Lizzie."

"What's up?" Winky said, after Kathy had left.

"Nothing."

"Come on. You look like you just lost a tin of salmon."

"I was meant to be buying a stupid Total Dream Office

for my niece, but I didn't get around to it, and now — "

"Total Dream Office?" He laughed. "I could have told you that you'd have to get in quick."

"How would you know?"

"Because I'm connected. Total Dream Office has been trending on Twitter for weeks now."

"Since when were you on Twitter?"

"Hey, just because I'm a cat doesn't mean I can't tweet. So what are you going to do?"

"Most likely die a slow, painful death at Kathy's hands."

Why wasn't I on Twitter? I would have known about Total Dream Office.

My phone rang, and Winky went back to his milk.

"Jill? Are you there?"

"Jack? Sorry. I was miles away."

"Sounded like it. Look, I just thought I'd give you a call to see if you wanted to get lunch some time before Christmas — if we can get a table that is. I'm going back home to see the family on Christmas Eve."

"Sure, I'd like that. I can make the day after tomorrow, and there's a place I know that should be able to squeeze us in. I'll get Mrs V to make a booking and let you have the details."

"Sounds great. I'll see you then."

Detective Jack Maxwell and I had a kind of on-off relationship. In truth, it was more off than on. Still, I lived in hope.

Mrs V was scowling when I went through to the outer

office.

"What's wrong?"

"It's your grandmother."

I might have known. "What's she done this time?"

"Kathy must have told her about the children's home project. She called just now to say she wants to get involved."

"Oh dear."

"You can say that again. You know what she's like. She always wants to take over. She said she'd be around later."

That sounded like my cue to leave.

"Will you have time to call Temperature?" I said.

"Do you want me to book a table for you?"

"Yes please. A table for two—around one the day after tomorrow. Then will you let Maxwell know once it's booked?"

"Nice to see that you two have got together in time for Christmas."

"We aren't together. It's just lunch."

"If you say so, dear. You *will* make an effort with your appearance, won't you?" I could feel her eyes look me up and down. "Something a little more daring on the neckline, maybe?"

"Maybe."

What on earth was I going to do about the stupid Total Dream Office? There had to be one in Washbridge somewhere, and if there was I'd find it.

***

Three hours later, and my feet were killing me. I must

have been in every toy shop in Washbridge, as well as most of the department stores. I'd received a mixed reception. Some people had been sympathetic to my plight — others had laughed in my face. I'd really blown it this time. Lizzie would hate me, and Kathy would most probably kill me.

Hold on a minute! What's that? It can't be, can it?

I'd almost forgotten about Tilleys Department Store. It was one of the oldest shops in Washbridge, and one of the most run-down. I couldn't remember the last time I'd been in there. But there — right there in the window was a solitary box. A box with the words 'Total Dream Office' on the front in bright, luminous letters.

I ran so fast that I got caught up in the revolving doors for a few moments. It would be just my luck to get to the counter as someone else bought the stupid toy.

"Yes, madam?" A middle-aged woman with the smallest ears I'd ever seen, greeted me.

"Total Dream Office," I shouted.

She took a step back — obviously terrified at the mad woman in front of her.

"Sorry." I tried to catch my breath. "Total Dream Office, please."

"We've sold out. I'm sorry."

"There's one there." I pointed to the window behind her. "Look!"

"Display only, sorry."

"I don't mind. I'll take it anyway."

"It's for display purposes only. I can't sell —"

I'd had enough. I cast the 'sleep' spell, and she slumped down onto the counter. I did a quick check to make sure there was no one watching—I needn't have worried because the store was deserted as usual—then I climbed into the window and grabbed the box.

"Yes!" I shouted, and gave a fist pump, much to the surprise of an elderly couple who were walking past the window.

It's not like I'd stolen it because I left the cash under the hand of the assistant who would have woken up by the time I was back on the street.

I'd done it. I'd never had a moment's doubt. Christmas shopping—pah! What was all the fuss about?

Chapter 4

This time, I was determined to catch Luther Stone under the mistletoe—if it was the last thing I did. But first, I had to silence that stupid cat. I know what you're thinking, but for once it *wasn't* Winky who was driving me insane. Ever since I'd got back to the flat, I'd had to put up with a stupid cat howling its head off.

I'd assumed the noise was coming from outside, but it actually got quieter when I stepped out of the building. It must be inside one of the flats. Maybe someone had gone out and left it without food? I went back inside, and followed the sound. I was getting closer now—it seemed to be coming from inside Betty Longbottom's flat. I'd no idea she even owned a cat.

I knocked on the door. The howling stopped immediately. I must have spooked it.

"Hello? Hello in there?"

The door opened, and Betty gave me a puzzled look. "Jill? Are you okay?"

"Fine yeah. I was just looking for the cat."

"Which cat?"

"Haven't you heard it? The stupid thing has been howling its head off for the last hour. It's been driving me mad. I thought it was coming from inside your flat."

"There's no cat in here."

"You must have heard it though?"

She shook her head. "I haven't heard anything, but then I have been practising for the carol service."

"Carol service?"

"Yes."

"You were singing?"

"Yes. Jill are you sure you're okay?"

"Err—yeah—err—I'm fine. Sorry to have interrupted you."

"No problem. I'd better get back to my practice."

And so she did, and the howling started up again. Anyone know where I can get some earplugs?

Yes! Yes! Yes! Luther was walking down the corridor towards me. I smiled my cutest smile, and glanced up at the mistletoe. I could almost feel those lips on mine. This was it! Christmas had come at last.

"Jill!"

I turned around to find Mr Ivers, my boring neighbour, standing behind me. He glanced at the mistletoe and smiled. Noooo! This could not be happening. But it was. Before I could object or kick him in the groin, he'd planted a big sloppy kiss on my lips. Luther grinned at the two of us as he walked past. Fantastic! I might as well rip the stupid mistletoe down for all the good it had done me.

I'd decided to take a quick look at the Total Dream Office—partly because I wanted to make sure the display unit hadn't been damaged, but also to find out what all the fuss was about.

"No! No!" This could *not* be happening. I'd thought the box was light, but then everything was made of plastic these days wasn't it? It turned out that my Total Dream Office wasn't made of plastic. My Total Dream Office was made of brown paper. In fact, my Total Dream Office was *just* brown paper—that's all there was inside the box. The display unit was just a box filled with brown paper. I didn't know whether to laugh or cry. Strike that—I knew exactly what to do.

Beg for mercy.

I made the call.

"Kathy. How are you?"

"What have you done, Jill?"

"What do you mean?"

"The only time you ask how I am is when you've done something."

"That's not true."

"Have you done something?"

"No."

"Are you sure? You don't sound very sure."

"It's more something I *haven't* done."

"What *haven't* you done, Jill?"

"Promise you won't be angry."

"I *will* be angry if you don't tell me right now."

"It's the Total Dream Office."

"Don't tell me you've dropped it. I warned you it was fragile."

"No. It's not that. I *kind of* don't have *all* of it."

"What do you mean? You aren't making any sense. What bit of it *do* you have?"

"The box."

There was the longest silence. I could almost feel her anger through the airwaves.

"What happened to the rest of it?"

"It—err—I—err—it—err—"

"Jill!"

"I didn't actually buy one until today."

"You told me you'd bought it weeks ago."

"I was mistaken."

"Mistaken?" She was shouting now. "You mean you

lied."

"A little."

"Either you lied or you didn't. You can't lie a 'little'. So where's the one you bought today?"

"It was ex-display. But when I got it home there was only brown paper in the box."

"They sold you brown paper?"

"They didn't exactly sell it to me."

"Don't tell me you stole it?"

"Of course not. Well, not exactly. The assistant fell asleep, so I took it. But I left the money!"

"Great! That's just great! Well congratulations, Jill. You have single-handedly wrecked your niece's Christmas. I hope you're proud of yourself."

"But, Kathy—"

She'd hung up.

Why was I such a terrible person? All I'd had to do was buy one toy. I was beyond stupid. How could I go to Kathy's on Christmas Eve now? Lizzie would hate me forever.

I didn't sleep well that night. I tossed and turned, thinking about what I could do to make it right, and came up with a big fat nothing. Still, even though I couldn't make things right with Kathy and Lizzie, there was still one person I *could* help.

***

"What's that?" Barry said. He was still under the bed.

"It's a sledge."

"Can I eat it?"

"No. It's for you to ride on."

"Cool." He crawled out from under the bed, and jumped onto the sledge. "It isn't moving."

"We have to take it outside."

"Don't like the white."

"I know. That's why I bought the sledge. You sit on this and I'll pull you."

"What about the white?"

"You don't need to touch the white—err—I mean snow."

"Promise?"

"I promise."

Barry looked a little apprehensive at first, but after a while he sat back and began to enjoy the ride. I'd asked the twins to come with us, but they were busy in the shop.

"Can we go to the park?" Barry said.

"That's where we're going. Don't you recognise this route?"

"Everything is white."

He was right—everywhere did look different covered in snow. It was beginning to look as if I'd get *one* white Christmas at least.

"Is it white in the park?" Barry said.

"It's white everywhere."

"Don't like the white."

I'd assumed that the snow would mean the park would be quieter than usual. Quite the opposite. It was full of kids sledging: Youngsters with their parents and older kids showing off to one another. We'd entered the park by a gate which was half way up the hill. That was my first mistake—I should have walked to the gate at the top of the hill, but Barry was quite a weight to pull, and I'd been hoping to get a rest. My second mistake was not staying close to the wall once we were in the park.

I didn't notice the sledge hurtling towards us until it was too late. In a panic, I leapt to one side as it came whizzing past.

"That was close." I turned around. Oh no! "Barry! Come back!"

In my panic I'd let go of the rope. Barry plus sledge were now careering down the slope.

I was already covered in snow, and I fell twice more as I chased after him. My boots were full of snow, and it was beginning to melt. The last I saw of Barry was when the sledge crashed through a clump of bushes. If he was hurt, I'd never forgive myself. As I scrambled under the bushes, snow fell off the leaves and down my neck. My hands were so cold that I could barely feel them.

"Barry! Barry! Where are you?"

After a couple of minutes, I spotted the sledge. It had come to rest next to a tree. But where was Barry?

"What are you doing in there, Jill?" a familiar voice said.

I crawled out from under the bushes to find Drake with a huge grin on his face.

"I've lost Barry."

"He's over there—with Chief."

I followed Drake's gaze, and sure enough there were Barry and Chief, Drake's dog, chasing one another around in circles.

"But, he's scared of the white—I mean snow."

"He doesn't look very scared."

Drake was right. Barry was having the time of his life.

"Are you okay?" Drake said. "You look frozen."

"That dog will be the death of me."

"I'd invite you back to my place to warm up, but there's somewhere I have to be in a few minutes."

"That's okay." I tried not to show my disappointment.

"I'll be in Washbridge tomorrow though. Maybe we can do lunch if we can get in anywhere?"

"That would be nice." What? Why shouldn't I have lunch with two different men on consecutive days? I was a free agent. Don't judge. "I know a restaurant where we'll be able to get a table."

Drake called Chief, and the two of them set off home. I called Barry. Then I called him again. And again. An hour later, I finally managed to get him back on the lead.

"I like white now," he said.

"So I see. Do you want to get back on the sledge?"

"No. I'll walk. I like white."

"What happened to you?" Amber giggled.

"Don't ask." My teeth were chattering.

"I thought Barry didn't like the snow." Pearl giggled too.

"Apparently, he loves it now."

"What about you?" Pearl said.

"I never want to see snow again as long as I live."

I took a nice hot shower, and treated myself to a latte and a blueberry muffin — a small one which had somehow been mislabelled 'large'.

Amber was busy behind the counter, but Pearl came to join me.

"Sorry for laughing earlier," she said, sheepishly.

"That's okay." It was easier to see the funny side now I

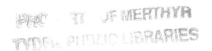

wasn't suffering from frost bite. "Anyway, it wasn't all bad. I ran into Drake. I'm seeing him for lunch tomorrow in Washbridge."

"That's great. Do you think you and he might become an item?"

I shrugged. "Who knows?"

For someone with no love life my love life was getting rather complicated. Drake tomorrow and Jack Maxwell the day after.

***

I wasn't sorry to see the back of the snow. Back in Washbridge, the temperature was several degrees higher, and there was no white to be seen. I called Mrs V to ask her to book me another table at Temperature for my lunch date with Drake.

I'd no sooner finished the call than my phone rang. It was Kathy—no doubt about to give me even more grief. I thought about letting it go to voicemail, but she would know I was ignoring her, and was likely to turn up on my doorstep. At least she couldn't hit me or throw anything at me over the phone.

"It took you long enough to answer," she said.

We were off to a good start.

"Sorry, I was—"

"Never mind. I need a favour and you don't get to say no because you owe me big time for spoiling my little girl's Christmas."

"Don't say that, Kathy. I feel bad enough as it is."

"Good. And so you should. She's going to be inconsolable come Christmas morning. Just thank your lucky stars you won't be there to see it."

"You won't tell her it was my fault will you?"

"Of course I will. You don't think I'm going to take the blame do you? Anyway, about this favour which you've agreed to."

Chapter 5

"Why do I have to go?" Mikey whined.

"Because I say so," Kathy said.

Wow, that old fall-back. My sister had finally turned into our parents.

As a favour to Kathy, or rather as my punishment, I'd agreed to take Mikey to see Santa at one of the major department stores. Lizzie had already paid him a visit, and delivered her Christmas list which, as Kathy had made a point of telling me, had Total Dream Office at the top.

"Santa isn't real," Mikey said. "It's just a man wearing a white beard."

"He is real," Lizzie yelled at him. "He's bringing me Total Dream Office."

Kathy glared at me—like I didn't already feel bad enough.

"You only think he's real because you're a baby!" Mikey teased his sister.

"I'm not a baby. I'm five!"

"Stop arguing you two." Kathy stepped between the kids. "You are going with Auntie Jill to see Santa, and that's all there is to it."

"Do you believe in Santa, Auntie Jill?" Mikey said.

"Me? Err—yes."

"Very convincing," Kathy whispered in my ear.

"I'm doing my best here," I whispered back. "It's not my fault that he doesn't believe in Santa."

"No, but it'll be your fault that Lizzie doesn't when he fails to deliver Total Dream Office."

Mikey had a long face on the drive into town. My numerous attempts at starting a conversation were met with silence or a grunt.

"Have you brought your list for Santa?"

"No."

"How will he know what to bring you?"

"Jack Brownlaw saw his dad bring his presents into his room last Christmas."

"How did he know it was his dad? It might have been Santa."

"Because his dad only has one leg."

"Right. Maybe his dad was helping Santa."

Mikey sighed, rolled his eyes and then turned to stare out of the side window. If I was going to redeem myself in Kathy's eyes, I had to turn this around. I had to convince Mikey there really was a Santa.

Grimshaws was the largest department store in town. My adoptive parents used to take Kathy and me there to see Santa when we were kids. I'd believed in him until I was eight years old—long after most of the other kids. That reminded me—Kathy had given up on Santa before she was five, so she had a nerve expecting Mikey to still believe.

Are you kidding me?

The queue wound all the way around the toy department and into the carpet section which shared the same floor.

"Do we have to wait?" Mikey complained.

"Yes, I promised your mum."

"It's at least an hour's wait," the woman directly in

front of us said. She had two young girls about the same age as Lizzie.

"Sorry?"

"They came around and told us there was a one hour wait from here."

Great.

"This is Sadie and this is Cindy." She introduced her daughters who both giggled. They were like miniature versions of the twins.

"Santa isn't real," Mikey blurted out.

The two girls immediately began to cry. Their mother gave me such a look.

"I'm sorry," I said, but she'd already moved a few feet away.

"Mikey. You mustn't say that. You'll upset the other children."

"Why not? It's true."

This was going to be a very long hour.

It was. In fact, it was a very long hour and a half. Santa was apparently on a go-slow. Still, the end was in sight. We were only a few feet away from the entrance. Santa's little helper, an elf, was taking the children's names. As we got nearer, I caught a glimpse of his face.

"Blaze?"

Blaze worked alongside Daze. They were sup sups (short for Super Supernaturals). They worked as RRs (short for Rogue Retrievers). Essentially, they went after supernaturals who had broken the sup code of ethics, and returned them to Candlefield.

"Hi, Jill. What are you doing here? I didn't know you had kids."

"I don't. This is Mikey. He's my sister's boy."

Blaze smiled at Mikey. Mikey scowled.

"More to the point, what are *you* doing here?" I said in a whisper to Blaze.

"We're on the trail of a rogue wizard. Long story — I'll fill you in some other time."

"Where's Daze?"

"Not far away." He glanced at the grotto. "Looks like it's your turn now."

I grabbed Mikey's hand and pulled him into Santa's Magic Kingdom which looked like it might fall down if there was a stiff breeze.

It was quite dark inside. Small red lights, embedded into the floor, marked a pathway to a gold throne on which was seated Santa.

"Ho, ho, ho!" He greeted us. His voice wasn't as deep as I'd expected it to be. "Who have we here?"

"This is Mikey." I gave my nephew an encouraging nudge in the back.

"Welcome to my magical kingdom, Mikey. Come and sit next to me, and tell me what you want me to bring you for Christmas."

Why did that voice sound familiar?

I nudged Mikey forward, but he refused to sit next to Santa.

"And what would you like for Christmas, young man?" Santa leaned forward in his chair.

"You're not Santa!" Mikey yelled, as he pulled at the beard.

I'm not sure who was more shocked. Mikey stood open-mouthed for a few seconds before screaming, "You're a lady!" Then he ran out of the grotto.

"Daze?" I stared in disbelief, as Daze reattached her beard. "Santa? Really?"

"Not my finest hour, I'm afraid," she said. "I hope I haven't upset the little man."

"I'd better go and find him. Catch you later."

I eventually tracked down Mikey in the toy car section. I bought him three new cars on the promise that he wouldn't tell his mum what had happened. What? I'm not above bribery, and besides it was a small price to pay to keep Kathy off my back.

"Mum!" Mikey yelled. "I told you Santa wasn't real. It was a lady with a false beard."

So much for the bribe.

Kathy glared at me — again. "Where did you take him?"

"To Grimshaws."

"Why do they have a woman dressed as Santa?"

"I don't know. You can't blame me for that. And anyway, why shouldn't a woman be Santa?"

Kathy sighed and went off after Mikey.

Another successful mission under my belt.

***

I decided to drop by the office to offer moral support to Mrs V and her yarnies. I was about to cross the road when I noticed a huge banner which had been strung across the front of the building: 'Every Child Deserves A Sock - The EAWM Charitable Foundation.'

What was going on?

My outer office was even more crowded. As well as the yarnies, there was a film crew from Wool TV. Standing centre stage was Grandma who appeared to be giving an interview to a young female reporter. I managed to make my way through the crowd to Mrs V.

"What's going on?"

"What do you think? Your grandmother has taken over as usual. She turned up with the radio and TV crews in tow."

"How come you aren't doing the interview?"

"Grandma insisted it was more important that I stick with the knitting."

"Who are the EAWM Charitable Foundation? You didn't mention them before."

"Haven't you figured it out? It's Ever A Wool Moment. I think your grandmother just made up the foundation."

I should have known. Anything for publicity — that was Grandma.

"Jill! Come over here!" Speak of the — Grandma was beckoning me over to her. I didn't like the look of this.

"This is my granddaughter," Grandma told the interviewer. The camera was still rolling. "She has been kind enough to provide these premises for the event."

"What do you think of what EAWM are doing here today?" the reporter asked me.

"I think Mrs V and her yarnies — err — I mean friends — are doing a magnificent job."

"Yes, yes," interrupted Grandma. "And of course, EAWM have provided our world famous Everlasting Wool and One-Sized knitting needles."

"A magnificent gesture, Jill, wouldn't you say?" The reporter thrust the microphone at me.

"Amazing."

I eventually managed to fight my way through to my office.

"Do they want me to make an appearance?" Winky was desperate to get on TV.

"Unlikely."

"Why not? I'm the star around here."

"That may be true, but the article is about providing needy children with a sock for Christmas."

"Stuff the needy children. What about my movie career?"

"What movie career?"

"The one I'm going to have when a Hollywood producer sees my face on TV."

"I'm not sure Hollywood producers watch Wool TV."

"You'd be surprised. From what I hear, a lot of them are into knitting in a big way."

Who knew?

"I thought I'd find you hiding in here." Grandma barged into my office and slammed the door closed behind her. Winky jumped so much he almost fell off the leather couch.

"I'm not hiding," I said. "This is my office in case you hadn't noticed."

"You could have sounded a little more upbeat about the part the EAWM Charitable Foundation is playing here today."

I laughed. Big mistake.

"What's funny?" Her wart was glowing red.

"Nothing."

"Do you usually laugh at nothing?"

"I was just wondering when you dreamed up the

EAWM Charitable Foundation. Looks to me like an excuse to get publicity for the shop."

Foot, mouth—when would I ever learn?

"I'll have you know that I take the foundation's responsibilities very seriously."

"Really?"

"Yes, really. Why else do you think I would have donated the wool and the knitting needles?"

"So it has nothing to do with the publicity?"

"Of course not."

"Is that why you had that enormous banner printed and hung outside?"

"You have a lot of your mother in you. Darlene always had way too much to say for herself."

"Is there any wonder, mother?" My mother's ghost had appeared next to the sofa. Winky hissed, and dived under my desk.

"I might have known you'd show up." Grandma sneered. "You two." She pointed a crooked finger at us. "You're like two peas in a pod." She made to leave. "I don't have time to stand here and argue. I have a radio interview in a few minutes."

"She drives me crazy," I said to my mother once we were alone.

"Tell me about it. Just imagine having her for a mother."

"I'm glad I've got you." I smiled.

"That's sweet."

"Will you be at Aunt Lucy's for Christmas dinner?" I said.

She frowned. "I'm really sorry, Jill, but I promised Alberto we'd visit his family on Christmas Day. He doesn't ask much of me, and I felt—"

"It's okay, honestly. I understand."

"I do have a present for you though." She pulled a tiny gift-wrapped parcel seemingly out of thin air. "Here."

"Thanks."

"You can't open it until Christmas Day though. Promise?"

"I promise."

"Okay. Well I'd better get back. Alberto has some last minute shopping to do. Take care of yourself, and don't let Grandma wear you down."

"I won't. Thanks."

With that, she disappeared.

Although I'd made her a promise, I'd never been very good at the whole 'not opening presents' thing. When I was a kid, I used to search the house to try and find my Christmas presents. Maybe I could just sneak a peek.

"Oh no you don't!" My mother's voice came from nowhere.

Chapter 6

I woke up the next morning to find a thick covering of snow in Washbridge. Maybe I would get *two* white Christmases after all. Fortunately, I now had the 'Eskimo' outfit which Grandma had magicked for me. That reminded me—I still owed Grandma a favour. She'd never mentioned it since the day at Cuppy C, but I wasn't naive enough to believe she'd forgotten about it. You could be sure it would be something truly awful.

I'd already bought a model aeroplane for Mikey for Christmas, but I still had to get something for Lizzie. I really didn't want to have to ask Kathy, but what choice did I have? I gave her a call.

"It's me."

"Morning."

"Am I forgiven yet?"

"No."

Great.

"I still need to get Lizzie a present for Christmas," I said.

"I've already bought her something from you. An Angel Hairdresser Salon."

"That sounds good."

"It cost seventy pounds."

How much!?!?

"That's great. I'll let you have the cash. I guess she'll be pleased with that?"

"It's a poor consolation prize."

"Right. Sorry."

"Do you want to make up a little for the Total Dream Office?"

"Yes. What can I do?"

"Pete's away on his course, and I can't get the car out because of the snow. I can pick Lizzie up from school, but Mikey is finishing later than usual because it's his class's Christmas party. Could you go and collect him at about four?"

"Sure. No problem. I imagine he's excited about the party?"

"I think so, but Santa is going to be there, and you know how he feels about that. Especially after the Grimshaws incident."

"Don't worry. I'll collect him."

So, Santa was going to be at Mikey's class's Christmas party. Maybe this was my chance to redeem myself—at least a little.

***

I spent ages deciding what to wear for my lunch date with Drake. In the end, I went for a turquoise dress which I'd bought over a year before, but never actually got around to wearing. I managed to dig my car out in no time thanks to a little help from the 'power' spell. Sometimes I loved being a witch.

Temperature was a small restaurant which was hugely popular with young professionals. What? I'm young. And I'm definitely professional. It was the one place I knew I could always get a table. Simon, the owner, always held a few tables back for VIPs. Not that I was a VIP, but my dad had helped him out big time when Simon's original partner had been embezzling funds out of the business. Simon had told my dad he would always have a table for him, and he had extended that promise to me after my dad died.

When I arrived at the restaurant, Simon was standing just inside the door next to the young woman who was allocating tables.

"Hi, Simon." I managed as I struggled out of my Eskimo coat.

"Jill. Nice to see you. It's been a while."

"I've been quite busy." But mainly broke. "I have a table booked."

"So I see. I was just talking to Tanya about your booking."

Oh no. Don't tell me they don't have a table. "Is there a problem? My PA rang through the booking."

"We have the booking."

"So, what's wrong?"

"We actually have two bookings for you."

"That's right. One for today and one for tomorrow." I smiled. "I know it was a bit cheeky booking on two consecutive days."

"Actually no."

"No?"

"You have two bookings for today. But none for tomorrow."

"Two?"

He nodded.

"For today?"

He nodded. "The two gentlemen arrived within a few minutes of each other. We weren't sure what to do, so we put them on separate tables at opposite ends of the restaurant."

How on earth had that happened? Mrs V must have

been so stressed with her knitting project that she'd mixed up the days. Oh bum!

"Which one of them arrived first?"

"The gentleman seated over there—in the corner."

"Hi, Drake," I said.

"You're looking exceptionally beautiful today, Jill." He flashed his trademark smile.

"Thank you."

"Are you okay?" He looked concerned. "Your voice sounds a little rough."

I nodded. "Just a bit of a sore throat." In fact, I daren't speak any louder in case Jack heard me.

"How did you manage to get a table in here this close to Christmas?"

"The owner was a friend of my father's." I passed Drake one of the menus I'd collected from Simon. "Shall we order? I'm rather hungry."

I called the waitress—a young woman with a pleasant smile.

"Tomato soup for me, please," I said.

Drake ordered the same.

"What are your plans for Christmas?" Drake asked.

"Sorry. Would you excuse me for a minute? I have to—err—make a call."

"Sure."

I scuttled across the restaurant to a small booth at the opposite side.

"Jack. Sorry I'm late."

"No problem. I've only been here a few minutes. I'm surprised you managed to get a table here this close to

Christmas."

"The owner is a friend."

"Would you like a drink?"

I'd left my wine on the other table.

"Just water. Shall we order?"

I signalled to the same waitress. She gave me a knowing smile. "Tomato soup?"

"Err—yes, please."

Jack ordered the same.

"How's business?" He took a sip of wine.

"Quite good," I lied. "How about you?"

"Well, you know. I—"

"Sorry, Jack. I just remembered there's an urgent call I have to make."

"Oh? Okay."

"Your soup is getting cold," Drake said. He was halfway down his.

"Sorry about that."

The tomato soup was delicious. I'd just finished it when I spotted the waitress with two more soups—headed in the opposite direction.

"How's Barry?" Drake asked.

"He's got over his fear of snow. Talking of which, it looks like you brought the Candlefield weather with you."

"Tell me about it. I hate snow. I've promised to visit my mother on Christmas Day. I hope the roads have improved by then or I'll have to resort to magic."

At least now I knew there was no point in inviting him to Aunt Lucy's for Christmas dinner.

"Excuse me, Drake. I need the loo."

"Soup's just arrived," Jack said. "It's very good."

I took a slurp. "Delicious."

"Are you spending the Christmas break with Kathy?" he asked.

"Only Christmas Eve. I'm going to visit my other family on Christmas Day."

"Where is it they live again? Candletown?"

"Candlefield."

"I still haven't been able to figure out where that is."

"Up north." I'd made the mistake of mentioning Candlefield to Jack Maxwell before I realised that I had to keep such information from humans. "What about you?"

"I'm going back home to see my parents too. That's always assuming I can get there. The weather isn't looking too promising."

"I need the loo. Will you excuse me?"

"I think I'll go with the traditional turkey lunch." Drake had been studying the menu.

"I'll have the same." I caught the waitress's eye.

"You really must learn to relax more," Drake said. "It's the Christmas holiday. You should be winding down."

"I am relaxed."

"Really? You seem as tightly wound as a spring. Maybe if you turned off your phone?"

"I'd love to, but there's a couple of urgent cases I'm working on right now."

"Will you be in Candlefield over the Christmas break?"

"I'm having Christmas dinner at Aunt Lucy's."

"That'll be nice."

"Grandma will be there."

"Not so nice then."

"Maybe if we ply her with drink, she'll fall asleep." I twiddled the fork in my hand. "Sorry, I really need to check back with Mrs V."

"Oh?"

"I'll only be a minute."

I rushed back to Jack.

"Where did that come from?" Jack had a puzzled look on his face.

"What?"

"The fork?"

"This? Oh, I noticed the one they'd given me had a mark on it, so I picked up another while I was passing."

Jack eyed me curiously as I replaced the offending cutlery.

"Turkey lunch for me," he said, after a quick look at the menu.

"Same for me."

"I noticed a banner hanging from your office window this morning on my way over," he said.

"Mrs V is knitting socks for the local children's home. My grandmother has got involved, and her charitable foundation is sponsoring it."

"You never mentioned your grandmother had a charitable foundation."

"It's a recent development." I took out my phone, and stared at the blank screen. "Sorry. Urgent message. I have to deal with this. I'll only be a minute."

Turkey lunch was waiting for me back at Drake's table.

"Everything alright?" he said.

"Err—yes. I seem to have lost my fork." I signalled to

the waitress who by now was struggling not to laugh. "Could I get another fork?"

After two bowls of soup and two turkey lunches – I was well and truly stuffed.

"Drake, I'm really sorry, but I don't think I can face dessert. I'm feeling a little queasy."

"Oh dear." His concern made me feel even more guilty.

"Do you mind if we call it a day?" I said. "I'll have them put this on my tab."

"I won't hear of it. This is my treat. Shall I walk you back to your car?"

"No. No. It's okay. I'll be alright once I'm out in the fresh air. Have a great Christmas, and I'm sorry about this."

"Don't worry about it." I heard him say as I rushed back to Jack.

"I think I'm going to have the blueberry cheesecake," Jack said.

"Look, Jack. I'm feeling a bit queasy. I'm going to have to call it quits."

"Oh, alright. I'll come with you then."

"No, no. Please stay and order dessert. I'll be fine once I'm outside. Have a great Christmas, and don't worry about the bill. I'll see to it."

"Nonsense. This is my treat."

"Okay, thanks. Sorry again."

What a nightmare!

Once outside, I headed across the road and took shelter in the doorway of a vacant shop. From there, I could see inside the restaurant. Jack was standing next to the pay-desk. Moments later, Drake appeared behind him. Jack turned around and the two men stared at one another.

***

As I walked past Ever A Wool Moment, I noticed the posters in the window for 'Ever's' Christmas party. It didn't look like just any old party. Sure, there would be food, drinks, games and prizes. But the main attraction, according to the poster, was an appearance by Martin Laslo—last year's winner of the Talent Factor, the annual TV talent show. As you might imagine, I wasn't a fan of such shows, but Kathy was—big time. She insisted on telling me all about it—like I cared. And even worse, she showed me clips on YouTube. Anyhow, she'd been absolutely crazy for Martin Laslo. One day while I was at her house, Peter had a right go at her for sending sixty texts to vote for him. How on earth had Grandma got him to agree to appear at her Christmas party?

Chapter 7

The TV and radio crews had left, and so had half of Mrs V's yarnies. She looked tired and drawn.

"Are you okay?"

"I'm worried we might not make the target. I don't want to let the kids down."

"I'm sure you'll do it. Where have the others gone?"

"Not everyone is used to marathon sessions like me. Quite a few of them have ailments, so they can't keep up the pace for too long." She sighed. "What will I tell the people at the children's home if we don't make it?"

"Don't worry about that. Just concentrate on your knitting. You still have plenty of time."

"You could join us," she said. "You must be building up your knitting speed by now."

Mrs V had bought me a beginner's knitting kit some months ago. Rather than hurt her feelings, I'd lied and told her I was using it regularly at home. In fact, I'd only ever attempted it once, and I'd got into such a mess with dropped stitches that I'd vowed never to knit again.

"I'd love to, but I have too much on what with—err—this and—err—that. You know how it is."

She eyed me suspiciously. She knew as well as I did that I hadn't had a sniff of a case in weeks.

"Anyway, I'm just on my way to pick up Mikey from school."

"How is the little lamb? I bet he's looking forward to Santa coming, isn't he?"

"Sort of."

"Give him and Lizzie my love."

"Will do. Better dash."

"Jill! Hold on."

Almost made it.

"I meant to ask how your lunch date went with Detective Maxwell?"

"Great thanks." I didn't want to make her feel even worse by telling her she'd messed up the bookings.

***

This had better work. I'd parked in the school's car park and was waiting for the man who'd been hired to play Santa. If my calculations were correct, he should be arriving at any moment. It wasn't difficult to spot him. The first clue was his physique (or lack of it). He didn't need any padding to play the part. The second clue was the sticker in the back window of the car: *Nicholas Saint - professional Santa Claus*. What did he do the rest of the year, I wondered. Compile the naughty list perhaps?

He didn't hear me walk up behind him as he leaned into the back seat of his car. He was a big man, so I had to put extra effort into the 'sleep' spell. As he slumped onto the seat, I hoped the spell would last long enough so he didn't wake up until I was back. If I'd miscalculated, and he woke up before then, I'd really have some explaining to do.

I knew the party was in the hall, so I used the 'shrink' spell to sneak past security and into the main building. Back at full size, I faced a real test of my magic powers. I'd used the 'illusion' spell before, but usually only on one person at a time. This particular variation of the spell required I effectively create a mass illusion. That required a whole different level of concentration. I wasn't even sure if I was up to it. If I wasn't, I'd be found out very quickly.

There were about thirty children in the hall. I recognised them as the kids from Mikey's class—I'd seen them once before when I'd paid his class a visit to stop another boy from bullying him.

I closed my eyes, and focussed. When I was sure I was ready, I cast the spell. Now came the moment of truth.

"Ho, ho, ho!" I yelled, in my best fat man's voice.

The kids all fell silent. I studied their faces as I took a seat at the front of the hall. Someone had placed a sack full of tiny presents behind the seat.

"Merry Christmas, children!" I shouted.

"Merry Christmas, Santa!" the majority of kids called back. Their initial shock had been replaced by a look of sheer joy. I spotted Mikey. He was standing with three other boys. They weren't smiling. Instead, they were whispering to one another.

"Come and sit on the floor. When I call your name, come and collect your present, and tell me what you'd like for Christmas."

Just then, the door behind me swung open. My heart missed a beat as I wondered if the 'real' Santa had woken early. It was a young woman—no doubt one of the teachers. I had to act quickly, casting the spell as I turned to face her.

"Oh? Santa? I didn't realise you'd arrived." She gave me a nervous smile. "Would you like something to eat or drink?"

"No, thanks. I was just about to begin."

She nodded and backed out of the room.

There was a list of names on a type-written sheet which

had been tucked into the sack of presents.

"Helen Allan."

A young girl with pigtails and a missing front tooth, jumped to her feet, and rushed over to me.

"What would you like me to bring you on Christmas Day, Helen?"

"I want a Total Dream Office."

Don't we all?

"And a Smash Kids Jigsaw, and a—"

It took another five minutes for her to reel off the full list. I hoped her parents had plenty of money—they were going to need it. Half of the presents in the sack were wrapped in pink wrapping paper; the other half were wrapped in blue. Not very PC.

"There you go, Helen." I handed her one of the 'blue' presents. "Have a great Christmas."

I called each of the kids in turn. Some kids had a Christmas list as long as your arm, others had more reasonable expectations. One young girl wanted a real lion. I said I'd see what I could do.

"What's your name, little boy?"

"I'm not little. And my name is Jack Brownlaw."

This was the kid who'd convinced Mikey that there was no Santa. The kid who'd caught his father delivering the presents.

"What would you like for Christmas, Jack?"

"What do you care? You're just an ordinary man with a false beard."

There was a collective gasp from the other kids.

"Are you saying you don't believe in Santa Claus?"

"Yeah. There's no such thing. I saw my dad put out the toys last year."

"That's because I asked your dad to help. I'd twisted my ankle that day."

He laughed. He wasn't buying it. It was time to bring out the big guns.

"Why don't you believe I bring the presents?"

"Because you can't deliver them to everyone. It would take too long."

"I see. Well, you haven't taken into account the fact that I can be in more than one place at once."

Jack laughed again, but a little more nervously this time.

"Look!" I pointed to the back of the hall.

There was a huge gasp when the kids spotted the facsimile of me. I'd cast a second illusion spell to make them see another 'me'. The other 'Santa' waved at them.

"And over there!"

Another spell – another Santa. I wouldn't have been able to perform this kind of magic even a few weeks earlier. My powers were now starting to come into their own. By the time I'd finished, there were five other Santas standing around the edge of the hall.

"So, now do you see how I can deliver presents to all the children?" I said.

The whole class, including Jack Brownlaw, stared open-mouthed. I glanced over at Mikey – I could see in his eyes that my work was done.

After the last of the presents had been handed out, I made my way back to the car park. With a quick 'forget' spell, I sent Nicholas Saint on his way.

When it was time to collect Mikey, he came running out to greet me.

"Santa is real!" he yelled.

"I know. What made you change your mind?"

"I saw him. He can be in more than one place at the same time. Even Jack Brownlaw believes in him now."

"That's great, Mikey."

***

"I don't believe it," Kathy said, once Mikey had gone to play in his room.

"What?"

"The Santa at school seems to have convinced Mikey that he *was* real. I can't make head or tail of it. Something about multiple Santas. Whatever he did, I don't care. Mikey's going to believe in him for at least one more year."

"That's great. Have you heard from Peter? How's he getting on with his course?"

"It sounds like he's enjoying it. I'm a bit worried about the weather though."

"What do you mean?"

"The snow is even worse where he is. If it doesn't let up, he'll struggle to get home."

"He has to get home for Christmas."

"I told him that if he doesn't, he's a dead man. By the way, how did your lunch with Jacky Boy go?"

"Who's that?"

"Come on, you know who I mean. How did your date with Jack Maxwell go?"

Kathy didn't know about Drake, so I couldn't tell her what really happened.

"Not as well as I'd hoped."

"You didn't get drunk and make a fool of yourself again did you?"

"Of course I didn't. I was just a little err—distracted—that's all."

"Are you seeing him again over Christmas?"

"No. He's going back home to see his family. Look, I'd better be making tracks."

"Okay. See you on Christmas Eve then."

***

The snow had started to fall again. If it kept this up, there was a real possibility that Peter wouldn't get back. That was all we needed. It would be bad enough when Lizzie realised she hadn't got the present she'd had her heart set on. How would the kids take it if their Dad couldn't get home?

As I walked back along the high street, a giant ball of wool handed me a flyer advertising Martin Laslo at the Ever A Wool Moment Christmas party. Once again, Grandma had mobilised her marketing might. The high street was full of identical man-sized balls of wool, all handing out the flyers. Might she have overstretched herself this time? Martin Laslo had a massive following—at least according to Kathy. How would everyone fit into that tiny shop?

Chapter 8

This was it. This was my final shot at getting Luther under the mistletoe, and I was determined it would work. Anyone who saw me loitering in the corridor outside my flat would probably have thought I was up to no good.

And, they'd have been right. Snigger.

Mr Ivers appeared. He looked really excited.

"Good morning, Mr Ivers," I said.

"Morning, Jill."

"You look very pleased with yourself."

"I am. You'll never guess what's happened."

I was pretty sure I would. "What's that?"

"Look what I received in the mail just now." He handed me a card which looked quite familiar.

"Oh—you've won a prize."

"Isn't it great? I have to go and collect it from the Town Hall."

"What have you won?"

"It doesn't actually say, but it's quite valuable apparently."

"When did you enter the competition?"

"I didn't. All Washbridge residents were automatically entered. The winners were picked out by postcode, and mine came out!"

"That's fantastic. That's a nice early Christmas present for you. I guess you'll be out for a while then?"

"I guess so. I'll let you know what I've won the next time I see you."

"Okay. Bye."

One down, one to go.

Grandma's influence must be rubbing off on me. I was

turning into an evil witch. Oh, well. Needs must.

"Jill!"

"Good morning, Betty. You're up bright and early."

"I know. You'll never guess what's happened."

I just might. "What's that?"

"Look what I got in the post." She handed me an identical card.

"You've won a prize!"

I really should be on stage. Washbridge Amdram – watch out.

"I know. Isn't it exciting?"

"Very. When did you enter the competition?"

"I didn't. Apparently, all the addresses in Washbridge were entered automatically, and mine came out a winner."

"How lucky!"

"Yes, I'm just on my way to the Town Hall now to collect my prize."

"Do you know what you've won?"

"No, but it says it's valuable."

"You'd better hurry then."

"I will. I'll probably catch up with you later."

"Yeah. Do let me know what you've won."

"Okay, bye."

Two down. None to go. It's just you and me now, Luther.

I knew he'd show up sooner or later. Sure enough, after twenty minutes, I heard Luther singing. Any moment now, he'd turn the corner, and our eyes would meet. Then he'd see the mistletoe, and kiss me. Once he'd kissed me, he'd realise what he'd been missing, and ask me out on a date. After a few dates, we'd get engaged, and then married, and then—hang on—don't get too carried away, Jill.

He was walking towards me. Any second now he'd see the mistletoe, notice me, and bingo! Our fates would be sealed.

"Luther!" A voice came from behind me.

I spun around to see his assistant, Lucinda.

"Oh!" She giggled. "I see mistletoe."

No! That's *my* mistletoe. Leave it alone.

"Morning, Lucinda," Luther said.

What about me? I'm right here. Hello?

The two of them drew closer and closer, and then their lips met under the mistletoe. I stood there—like a spare part—just watching them. After their kiss, Luther turned to me and said, "Oh, hello, Jill. I didn't see you there."

Obviously.

"Come on, Luther, we're running late," Lucinda said. "We'd better hurry." Then she glanced at me. "Nice to see you again—err—Jill, isn't it?"

"Nice to see you too *Loo—sin—da*." Then she'd gone. They'd both gone. And with them, my last chance of getting a Christmas kiss from Luther Stone. My future was in tatters. My engagement, my wedding dreams and the children we would have had together—all gone.

Merry blooming Christmas.

***

It was the day of the Ever A Wool Moment Christmas party. I really wanted to give it a miss, but if I didn't turn

up, Grandma would be incandescent, and the consequences wouldn't be pretty. At least I wasn't going alone. I'd have Mrs V for moral support.

"What do you mean, you're not going?" I said.

"I can't, dear." Mrs V looked absolutely exhausted. She'd been knitting non-stop for hours. All of her yarnie friends had now gone home, unable to carry on a moment longer. So it was just Mrs V, at her desk, knitting as though her life depended on it. Her eyes were sunken, and her face was pale and drawn. She looked dreadful.

"Mrs V, you really should go home."

"I can't, dear. I made a promise to have the hundred socks ready in time for Christmas Eve. I can't let the children down."

"But you're going to make yourself ill."

"I can't let them down, Jill. I have to do it."

"I wish I could stay with you and help, but if I don't go to Grandma's Christmas party, she'll kill me — or worse."

"It's okay, dear. I understand. She'll probably have a go at me for not turning up, but I don't care. The children are more important than your Grandma and her silly party."

"I'd better be off," I said. "Take care, and when you reach the point that you can't do any more, please take a taxi home. I'll pay for it."

"I'll be fine. Go and enjoy your party."

Some chance.

***

I'd only gone a few yards along the high street when I noticed a long queue, which was made up predominantly of young women. The queue snaked around the corner and down towards Grandma's shop. I couldn't imagine what they could be queuing for. Then, when I got to the door of Ever A Wool Moment, I realised. They were all there for Grandma's Christmas party.

How had she managed to get Martin Laslo to appear at a Christmas party in a wool shop? Surely there must have been hundreds of venues who would have paid him a small fortune to appear. And, how were all these people going to get inside 'Ever'? More importantly, how was *I* going to get inside? Standing either side of the door were two burly security guards. They were checking tickets before allowing anyone in. And I didn't have one.

I started towards the door.

"You'll have to get to the back of the queue," said one of the security men.

"Yeah, what do you think you're doing?" shouted a girl at the front of the queue. "We've been waiting here for two hours. Get in line."

"But, it's my grandma's shop."

"No cutting in," someone else shouted.

Suddenly I realised that I had the perfect excuse to duck out. If they wouldn't let me in, what could I do? Oh well. Never mind.

"Let her in." Grandma's voice boomed. She was standing just inside the door. One of the security men beckoned me through.

"How come she gets in?" someone said.

"Yeah, why can she get in without a ticket?"

"I was beginning to think you weren't coming," Grandma said.

"I've been working," I lied.

"Priorities, young lady. Priorities. And where's

Annabel?"

"Mrs V can't come. She's still knitting socks for the children's home; they have to be ready for tomorrow. She's absolutely exhausted."

"Huh! Excuses, excuses. Some people just don't understand what's important."

Unbelievable.

"Anyway, I have things I have to attend to." She grumbled. "Go and see Kathy; she'll give you a drink." With that, Grandma disappeared into the crowd.

I managed to fight my way to where Kathy and three other people were serving drinks from behind a makeshift bar. I caught her eye, and she came over to me.

"This is madness!" she said. "Sheer madness. Did you see the queue outside? It stretches right around the block. It's been like that all day."

I glanced around. The shop was full, but it wasn't *that* full. "Where are they all?"

"I don't understand it." Kathy shrugged. "They've been coming in in droves for ages, but the shop doesn't seem to get any fuller."

It didn't make sense—then the penny dropped— Grandma was obviously using magic.

"What time does Martin Laslo make his appearance?" I asked, after Kathy had handed me a drink.

"In about an hour. He seems like a nice young kid. He's in the back room. Come with me, and I'll introduce you."

"No, it's okay."

"Come on, Jill. It's less crowded in there."

She dragged me through to the back office, and sure enough, there was Martin Laslo.

"Martin, this is my sister, Jill Gooder."

"Pleased to meet you." Surprisingly, he seemed quite shy.

"This must be an unusual venue for you to play?" I said.

"Very. I used to play small clubs before I won Talent Factor, but I've never played in a wool shop before."

"I'm surprised you took the gig. Surely you could have been doing something more high profile?"

"I'm not sure how it happened. I don't remember agreeing to do it. I've spoken to my agent, and he doesn't have any recollection of it either. But there's a signed contract, so here I am, in a wool shop."

I knew it. Grandma had been at it again. She'd obviously used magic to get one of the country's top acts to appear in her shop. She was unbelievable. The woman had no shame, and showed a total disregard for the rule against flaunting magic in the human world. It was disgraceful, and something I'd never do — obviously.

I'd managed to get a good position at the front of the shop by the time Martin began his act. He was very talented, and gave a totally committed performance, even though he must have wondered why on earth he was there. The crowd loved him. The noise inside the shop was deafening. Everyone who'd been queueing, had managed to get in — somehow.

After a few drinks, Kathy and I really got into the spirit of it. We even managed to find a space where we could dance. By the end of the night, everyone had had a great time. I was shattered, and I'd probably had one drink too many, so Kathy and I shared a taxi. After I'd dropped her off, I went home to a good night's sleep.

Chapter 9

The next morning, I didn't wake until nearly ten o'clock—I wished I hadn't bothered. My head was thumping. I really shouldn't have had that last drink. I'd never admit it to Grandma, but it had been a great night. Whether it would result in more custom for Ever A Wool Moment, I wasn't sure, but all the newspapers would no doubt cover the event, and the publicity couldn't hurt.

I took two painkillers with a cup of tea. It was only then that I realised I hadn't checked in on Mrs V. The poor old dear had been dead on her feet when I'd left her. I should have called in the office after the party, but I'd been tired, and a little the worse for drink. I took a shower, got dressed, and made my way to the office as fast as I could. I just hoped she was okay.

As I approached the building, I could see the lights were on in the outer office. The poor old dear must have been there all night. I hurried upstairs, and found her fast asleep with her head on the desk. I tried to creep into my office without her hearing, but the door creaked and she stirred.

"Jill? Is it morning?"

"It's eleven o'clock, Mrs V."

"Oh no! I must have fallen asleep."

"You look terrible."

"I should have stayed awake. It was the only chance I had to get them done. Now I've let everyone down."

There were socks all over the floor.

"How many have you done?"

"I don't know. I lost track. I seem to remember I'd done ninety, and I had another ten to do, but then I must have fallen asleep."

"Let's get them all together and count them. There may be more than you think."

Mrs V was too tired to do anything, so I gathered up all the socks from the floor. Sure enough, just as she'd said, there were ninety of them.

"What about those over there on top of the filing cabinet?" I said.

She looked round in a daze. "Where did they come from?"

I walked over to the cabinet, picked up the socks, and counted them. "There's another ten here. That makes a hundred. That's what you needed, isn't it?"

"Yes—but—where did those last ten come from?"

"They look the same as the others to me."

"But I didn't put any over there."

"I'm not sure you knew *what* you were doing. You were practically knitting in your sleep."

"You're probably right, dear." She seemed much brighter now she realised that she'd actually achieved the target. "Let's get them into a bag," she said. "I have to deliver them to the children's home."

"You're not in a fit state to go anywhere."

"But I have to. I'm fine."

"Well, at least let me book a taxi to take you there, and then to take you home."

"Okay, thank you, dear."

I put the socks into a bag, and carried them downstairs where we waited together for the taxi to arrive. Once I'd waved her off, I made my way back upstairs. I had a feeling there was something fishy going on.

As soon as I walked into my office, Winky was on at me.

"Do you know what time it is? I'm starving."

"I slept in."

"What a surprise. Were you drunk again?"

"No—I only had a—"

"That's what I thought. Drunk again."

"It was a Christmas party. Everyone has a drink at a Christmas party."

"Has the old bag lady gone? She's been here all night."

"She was busy."

"I know. I heard all about it. Anyway, she got the hundred done, didn't she?"

"Yeah, how did you know?"

He smirked.

"Did you have something to do with those ten socks on the filing cabinet?"

"I might have."

"What did you do?"

"I could see the old bag lady was never going to make it. I'm not heartless, and it *is* Christmas after all. I didn't like to think about those poor kids with no sock for Santa to put their presents in."

"But how did you get them done in time? Can you knit?"

"Do I look as though I can knit?"

I wouldn't put anything past Winky. After all, he was a master of semaphore, could fly a remote control helicopter and was an expert darts player. Anything was possible.

"Yes?"

"Of course I can't. I just searched online until I found

socks which were a close match to those the old bag lady was knitting. I had them sent by courier. The old bag lady was asleep when they arrived."

"That must have cost a pretty penny."

"Yeah, but *you* paid for it, so it doesn't matter."

I might have known—still, never mind—it was for a good cause.

"Now, is there any danger of getting any food around here?"

***

By mid-afternoon, I'd started to come around. I still couldn't get over what Winky had done for Mrs V. He really was a dark horse. For all that he insisted he hated the 'old bag lady' as he always referred to her, he'd been there for her when she'd needed help. She'd have been devastated if she'd let down the kids at the children's home.

Mrs V had called me when she got home to let me know that she was okay. Apparently the children were delighted with the socks. I was pleased to hear that she'd be spending the holiday season with some of her yarnies. I'd been a little concerned that she'd be alone, or worse still, stuck with her sister, Mrs G.

Normally I'd have been looking forward to spending Christmas Eve at Kathy's, but I knew I was still in the bad books because I'd failed to buy the Total Dream Office. I felt really awful that Lizzie would wake up on Christmas morning only to find that Santa hadn't brought her the present she'd wanted so much. If Kathy had a go at me, I'd just have to take it on the chin. I deserved it.

My phone rang. It was Kathy.

"Everything okay?" I said.

"No, everything isn't okay. Pete's stuck."

"What do you mean?"

"He can't get back from his training course. They're snowed in. The roads are all blocked."

"Can't he get a train?"

"He just rang from the railway station. Because the roads are blocked, everyone is having to use the railway, so the trains are all full. He can't get one until Boxing Day."

"What?"

"He's stuck there until Boxing Day."

"That's terrible."

"Tell me about it."

"Have you told the kids?"

"No, not yet. It's going to be a *fantastic* Christmas. Not only is Lizzie not going to get the present she's been wanting for months, but now their daddy's not going to be here." She sighed. "I assume you're still coming over?"

"Yeah, of course. The roads are pretty bad here, but they are passable. It must be a lot worse where Peter is."

"Yeah, they've had a lot more snow there apparently. Anyway, I thought I'd better let you know." Kathy sounded resigned. "I'll see you later."

"Kathy, which station is he at?"

"He's at Westhorpe, why?"

"No reason. I just thought I might give them a ring to see if there's anything I could do."

"There's nothing anyone can do, Jill. He's stuck. The roads are blocked. The trains are full. Game over! I'll see you later."

Kathy was wrong. There *was* something I could do.

I closed my eyes, focussed as hard as I could, and magicked myself across the country. I landed smack bang outside Westhorpe railway station. The snow was at least eighteen inches deep—way deeper than in Washbridge. No wonder the roads were blocked. It was pandemonium inside the station. People were shouting, pointing at notice boards, and berating staff. I wasn't sure if I'd even find Peter, and then it occurred to me that I could phone him.

"Hello?"

"Peter, it's Jill."

"Oh? Hi, Jill. Did Kathy tell you what's happened?"

"Yeah. It sounds pretty bad over there."

"It is. The roads are impassable, and the trains are all full. It looks like I'm stuck here until Boxing Day."

"That's terrible."

"Don't worry about me; I'll be fine. Make sure the kids have a good Christmas. You'll have to be Santa Claus."

"Whereabouts are you, Peter?"

"I'm at the station."

"Yeah, I know. But where *exactly* in the station are you?"

"In the waiting room, next to the café. Why?"

"Oh, no reason. I just wondered if you'd managed to find a seat."

"Not exactly. It's jam-packed in here. I'm sitting on the floor, but at least it's warm and dry."

"Okay, Peter. I'm really sorry. See you soon."

"See you, Jill. Merry Christmas."

"Merry Christmas, Peter."

I looked around and quickly spotted the café. I fought my way over there, and sure enough, next to it was the waiting room. I glanced through the window, and spotted Peter in one corner. He looked miserable—like everyone else in there. I made my way over to him, trying not to step on any of the people sitting on the floor.

"Jill?" Peter said. "How did you—?"

"Don't ask questions. Just come with me."

He was so shocked to see me there that he picked up his bags, and followed me out of the waiting room. I hurried ahead; I didn't want to give him a chance to ask awkward questions. Once we were outside, I found a quiet spot.

"What's going on?" he said.

I grabbed his hand, cast the spell, and moments later, we were outside Washbridge railway station.

"What just happened?" Peter looked around in a daze.

"Come with me." I led him to one of the taxis in front of the station.

Before he could object, I'd pushed him and his luggage inside. He wound down the window, obviously still disorientated.

"Jill? What's happening? I don't—"

I cast the 'forget' spell, and told the taxi driver to take him home.

Chapter 10

I hadn't been back at my flat very long when my phone buzzed with a text. I assumed it would be Kathy informing me that Peter had made it home, but the sender's number was unrecognised.

The message was brief, but chilled me to the bone.

I believe you are looking for me.
I'm in your office right now.
TDO

The Dark One — the most powerful and evil of the sups.

I'd tried so hard to find any information on him with little or no success. Why had he chosen to contact me now? No one knew *who* or even *what* he was — did he really intend to reveal himself to me? And if he did, would he let me live to tell the tale? Maybe I should contact someone — but who? Did I really want to put someone else in harm's way too? No — I had to do this alone.

I didn't dare allow myself time to think — if I had, I might have lost my nerve. I hurried over to my office as quickly as I could.

The outer office was in complete darkness when I let myself in. There was just a dull light coming from my office — the one I'd left on for Winky.

Winky! Oh no! If TDO had harmed my darling cat, I'd — I'd — I'd do something unspeakable. I burst through the door — my heart was racing.

Winky looked up from his saucer of milk. "You scared

me to death!" he said, as he licked his lips.

He looked okay, but where was TDO? I glanced around the room; there was no one else in there.

"Are you okay, Jill?" Winky jumped onto the sofa.

"Shush!" I whispered. "We're in danger."

"From what?"

"Have you seen anyone?"

"Not a soul. It's been lovely and peaceful for a change." He scratched his ear. "I take it you got my text."

"Text? What text?"

"Isn't that why you're here?"

"Hang on. You sent me a text?"

"Yeah." He pointed to a large bag on the floor near to the desk.

"What is it?"

"Jeez. How on earth do you make a living as a P.I.? I told you in the text—it's the TDO."

"Huh?"

"Oh boy." He rolled his one eye. "Total Dream Office. That's what you were trying to find isn't it?"

Total Dream Office? TDO? Of course!

"You found one? How?"

"I've told you before. I have skillz."

I rushed over to the box and looked inside. Sure enough there it was—the most sought after toy of the year.

"Winky, thank you. How much do I owe you?"

"You've already paid for it—I used your credit card."

I scooped him into my arms and gave him a hug.

"Put me down, woman. I don't know where you've been."

***

That evening, I felt on top of the world when I arrived at Kathy's house.

"Pete made it home." She beamed.

"Really?" I feigned surprise. "I thought he was stuck."

"I thought he was too. He'd told me there was no chance of getting a train."

"So, what happened? What changed?"

"I don't know, and neither does he. The only thing he can remember is getting a taxi from Washbridge station. He must have fallen asleep on the train."

"That's fantastic!"

Peter came to the door, and for one horrible moment, I thought he was going to remember.

"Hi, Jill," he said. "Come on through."

I followed the two of them into the living room. "Where are the kids?"

"They're in Lizzie's bedroom," Kathy said. "I bought them an extra present each which I've just given them. I figured that would keep them occupied, and give us a little peace and quiet."

"Good thinking," I said. "I'm glad you made it home, Peter."

"Me too, but I really don't know how I did it. I was sure all the trains were fully booked, and I was going to be stuck there until Boxing Day."

"Maybe they put on more trains?"

"They must have. I was so exhausted I must have fallen asleep on the journey home."

"Anyway," Kathy said. "What's in the bag?"

"I've got a surprise for you." I grinned.

"What kind of surprise."

"I can't show you in here. Let's go into your bedroom."

"Is it something for me?"

"No, it's not for you."

"I might have known."

I turned to Peter. "Can you make sure the kids don't follow us?"

"Yeah. No problem."

"I still don't understand how Pete got back here," Kathy said. "One minute he was telling me he was stuck, and the next he was at the front door."

"What does it matter? He's home for Christmas. Just be happy."

"You're right. Anyway, what have you got in there?"

I took the toy out of the bag and Kathy gasped.

"How? Where? When?" She stared at the Total Dream Office in disbelief. "I thought you hadn't got one."

"I hadn't until just now."

"But there aren't any to be had anywhere."

"I managed to find one."

"That's fantastic, Jill! Lizzie will be so pleased. It'll make all the difference to tomorrow morning. Thank you." She threw her arms around me and gave me a big hug. "I thought this was going to be the worst Christmas ever, but now Peter's home and you managed to get this— thanks!"

"Do I get a custard cream?"

"You can have the whole packet to yourself. Come on, I'll make us a cup of tea."

The evening was a delight. The kids were hyper and full of excitement, and everyone had a great time. When it was time for me to leave, we all wished each other a merry Christmas. I was so relieved that Lizzie would wake up in the morning to find that Santa had brought her the toy she'd had her heart set on.

***

The kids rang me ludicrously early on Christmas morning, but I didn't mind. It was great to hear their happy, excited voices.

"I got a motor racing set," Mikey said. "It's fantastic! It goes really fast. I like to be the blue car. Daddy's rubbish."

"I got Total Dream Office," Lizzie said. "It's brilliant! I knew Santa would bring it. Mummy said I mustn't be disappointed if he didn't, but I knew he would. I want to show it to you, Auntie Jill. Are you coming over today?"

"Not today. You're going to your grandma's, but I'll see you soon and you can show me then."

"Okay, bye. Merry Christmas!"

Kathy took the phone from Lizzie.

"Everything okay?" I asked.

"Couldn't be better. The kids are thrilled with their toys. You should have seen Lizzie's face when she saw the Total Dream Office. What about you? Are you sure you're going to be okay today?"

"Yeah, I've got one or two things planned. I'll be fine. You lot enjoy yourselves. I'll catch up with you tomorrow."

"Okay, then. See you. Merry Christmas."

"Merry Christmas, Kathy."

***

It was my first Christmas in Candlefield; my first Christmas with my new family. I'd been looking forward to it for quite some time.

"I don't know why you can't use magic," Grandma moaned. "Christmas dinner would have been ready by now."

Even on Christmas Day, some things never changed. I was at Aunt Lucy's. Everyone was there: the twins, their fiancés, Lester and of course my favourite family member, Grandma, who had been complaining for the last fifteen minutes.

"I've already told you, mother," Aunt Lucy said. "I am not using magic to make Christmas dinner. It doesn't taste the same."

"Of course it tastes the same—as long as you know what you're doing. I could have had this ready in two minutes."

"In that case, you should have stayed at home and made your own Christmas dinner." Aunt Lucy was getting angrier and angrier.

"I would have, but I know you all want me here."

We looked at one another. We were obviously all thinking the same thing, but no one dared say a word.

The twins pulled me to one side, and Pearl said, "We're going to make snowmen in the garden. Do you want to come and help?"

"No thanks. It's too cold for me out there. You're welcome to it."

"It'll pass the time until dinner is ready," Amber said. "Plus we'll get away from Grandma. Are you sure you don't want to join us?"

"Yeah, I'm sure. You go ahead. I'll watch you through the window."

The twins went outside, dragging their fiancés with them. Neither Alan nor William looked very enthusiastic, but they didn't seem to have a say in the matter.

I watched them as they rolled huge balls of snow. They were all laughing and making a terrible noise. They were obviously competing to see which couple could make the best snowman.

"What's wrong with those stupid girls?" Grandma said. "They're giving me a headache."

"It's called having fun," Aunt Lucy said. "Do you remember what that is? F U N?"

"That's not fun. That's noise."

The twins were in hysterics now. Grandma gave them a look, and I sensed she had cast a spell, but I wasn't sure which one until the clouds above the garden suddenly parted, and the sun appeared. The heat from the sun's rays began to melt the snowmen right before my eyes. The twins looked on in horror as their creations melted. No sooner had the snowmen disappeared than so did the sun. The sky was overcast again. Amber, Pearl and their fiancés all looked mystified. Grandma looked very pleased with herself.

Dinner was well worth the wait. It was delicious. There was turkey, Aunt Lucy's special mashed potatoes, five types of vegetable and gravy to die for. For dessert, there was an amazing caramel apple betty with cinnamon ice cream. We rounded it off with coffee. There wasn't a scrap of food left on anyone's plate. Even Grandma had enjoyed it, although she did manage to complain about the size of the portions. Everyone pulled a cracker; Lester almost fell off his seat when he pulled his with Grandma—she always seemed to get the gift inside.

After dinner, presents were handed out. I received a lovely pair of gloves, a pretty necklace, and a beautiful handbag.

"This is my present to you, Mum," Amber said.

"No, here. Open mine first," Pearl said, trying to push her sister out of the way.

"She wants to open mine first," Amber said.

"Girls, girls. It's not a competition." Aunt Lucy picked up both presents.

"Open mine first, please," Amber said. "You'll love it."

"You'll like my present more," Pearl said.

"Why don't I open them at the same time?"

"Okay then." Amber pouted.

"I suppose so." Pearl pouted too.

Aunt Lucy somehow managed to tear the wrapping off both presents at the same time. When the paper was removed it revealed two very similar, if not identical, red boxes.

"Interesting?" she said, as she opened the lids.

Everyone laughed except Amber and Pearl. William and Alan soon stopped when the twins gave them a look.

"Great minds think alike," Aunt Lucy said, staring at two identical pairs of earrings.

"You copied me again," Pearl said.

"I did not! I got mine first," Amber said. "You copied me."

"How was I supposed to know you'd got them?"

Aunt Lucy held up a hand to silence the squabbling. "They're beautiful. I love them both."

"Whose will you wear first?" Amber insisted. "Wear mine, please!"

"I bought them first," Pearl said. "You have to wear mine first."

"I'll tell you what I'm going to do. I'll wear one from each box."

After all of the presents had been opened, I went upstairs on the excuse of going to the loo. I wanted to be alone when I opened the present which my mother had given me. The gold locket was heart-shaped. Inside was a photo of a newly born baby, and it took me a few seconds to realise it was me.

"Are you okay?" Aunt Lucy said when I re-joined them.

"Yeah, I'm fine."

"Are you sure? Your eyes look a little red."

"I'm fine, honestly. I just had something in my eye."

Chapter 11

By early evening, I was full of mince pies and chocolate. Everyone was having a great time, mainly because Grandma had fallen asleep in the dining room, and we'd left her there. But, I was beginning to feel a little guilty. I knew Kathy, Peter and the kids would be having a good time, and that Mrs V was okay because she was spending Christmas with the yarnies. But what about Winky? The poor old thing was all by himself in my office. Even though he drove me crazy, I didn't like to think of him all alone on Christmas Day. I decided to pop over there for a few minutes to make sure he was okay. I told everyone that I'd only be gone for a short while, and then I magicked myself back to Washbridge.

I arrived just outside the building, and when I looked up I could see there were lights on in the outer office. They were changing from one colour to another: green, followed by red, then yellow, and then blue. What was going on?

I let myself into the building and made my way up the stairs. As I did, the sound of music got increasingly louder. What on earth was happening in there? The outer office was full of cats. They were dancing, laughing, drinking and eating. There must have been twenty of them, all in party gear. In one corner stood a record deck being operated by a cat in dark glasses who was speaking into a microphone. None of them seemed to take any notice of me as I made my way across the room. Then I felt a tap on my leg.

"What are you doing here?" Winky said. He was wearing a purple, sparkly suit with a matching eyepatch.

"What on earth is going on?" I shouted over the music.

"I can't hear you."

"Let's go through to my office." I pointed.

He followed me—it was still loud, but at least I could hear myself think.

"What's going on out there?"

"It's my Christmas party."

"You didn't tell me you were having a party."

"I didn't think I needed to. You saw me sending out the invitations."

"I thought those were Christmas cards."

"Nah, I don't bother with Christmas cards. Anyway, what are you doing here, Billy-No-Mates? Are you so desperate for company that you decided to gatecrash?"

"No! I was at my own Christmas party. I just wanted to check you were okay. But it looks like you're having a great time."

"How very sweet of you to care."

"There is one other thing while I'm here."

"Hurry up then. I've promised Bella a dance."

"I just wanted to say thank you."

"What for?"

"For buying the socks for Mrs V."

"It was nothing."

"And for finding the Total Dream Office."

"Not a problem. Anyway, if you want to show your gratitude, you know how to do it, don't you?"

I smiled. "Red, not pink?"

"Got it in one."

Winky was obviously okay. When I left, he was jiving with Bella. I magicked myself back to Aunt Lucy's where everyone except Grandma was in the living room.

"Is Grandma still asleep in the dining room," I said in a whisper. I didn't want to risk waking her up.

"No," Aunt Lucy said. "She's gone upstairs for a lie down."

We all settled down to watch Christmas TV. There's nothing better than mindless television, lots of chocolate and plenty of ginger beer. My idea of heaven.

"Jill!" A voice echoed above our heads.

Everyone looked at me.

"Jill, can you come up here?"

"Why is Grandma shouting me?" I looked to the others.

Everyone shrugged. They were just relieved that she wasn't calling them.

If I ignored her, perhaps she'd go away.

"Jill! Hurry up!"

"You'd better get up there, Jill." Amber giggled.

"Yeah, you don't want to keep Grandma waiting." Pearl giggled too.

I'd get them back for this.

I made my way upstairs — resigned to my fate.

"Where are you, Grandma?"

"In the front bedroom."

I knocked on the door.

"Don't hang around out there. Come in."

When I walked into the room, I found Grandma lying on the bed. She'd taken off her shoes and stockings. Her feet were even more horrible than her wizened hands.

"What can I do for you?"

"Do you remember you promised to do me a favour for kitting you out in winter clothing?"

"Err — yeah."

"Well, I think it's time for you to pay your debt."

"But, Grandma, it's Christmas Day."

"I know what day it is."

"What do you want?"

"My bunions are giving me a lot of gyp today. I'd like you to rub this ointment on them."

Oh bum!

A brief message from Winky

(SPOILER ALERT! Do not read this message until you have read the book)

A big hello to all you Winky addicts out there. I'm delighted to see that I've been given my own cover at long last—I look so much better in colour.

Incidentally, don't be fooled by what you have just read. Jill may think I've turned over a new leaf just because I helped the old bag lady with her sock woes, and found some stupid toy, but you and I know better. I'm playing the long game—that's what it's all about. A nod is as good as a Winky to a blind—you get my drift.

I feel I owe you all an apology for making you endure those boring stories about Jill Gooder in the Witch P.I. Mysteries. I know that you only put up with them so that you can get the occasional glimpse of *yours truly*. Believe me, I have tried to tell Adele that she should drop Jill, and instead write a series of books devoted just to me. The problem is that Adele isn't a witch, so she can't understand a single word I say. Maybe I'll write my memoirs—that is sure to be a best seller.

Finally, and most importantly, I would like to wish you all a Merry Christmas and a Happy New Year. Please do not spend too little on my present, and just remember—it's red not pink.

ALSO BY ADELE ABBOTT

The Witch P.I. Mysteries:

See web site for availability.

The Susan Hall Mysteries:
Whoops! Our New Flatmate Is A Human.
Whoops! All The Money Went Missing.
Whoops! There's A Canary In My Coffee
See web site for availability.

AUTHOR'S WEB SITE
Http:www.AdeleAbbott.com

FACEBOOK
http://www.facebook.com/AdeleAbbottAuthor

MAILING LIST
(new release notifications only)
http:/AdeleAbbott.com/adele/new-releases/

Printed in Great Britain
by Amazon